CHARACTER SHEET

LIFE   16

DISGUISE

WEAPON THROWING

BURGLARY

ITEMS

POISONS
FEMME FATALE   DOSES 1
BLACK LOTUS   DOSES 1

HEALTH POTIONS
DOSES   3

DRINK A DOSE FOR +3 LIFE

INVENTORY

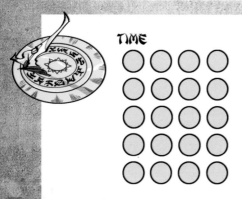

TIME

○ ○ ○ ○
○ ○ ○ ○
○ ○ ○ ○
○ ○ ○ ○
○ ○ ○

NOTES

HOW TO PLAY

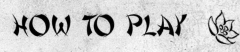

YOU PLAY THE ROLE OF A YOUNG BOUNTY HUNTER WITH AN ARRAY OF DANGEROUS TALENTS, NECESSARY FOR SURVIVING IN SUCH A HAZARDOUS LINE OF WORK. PROOF OF YOUR REPUTATION AND EFFICIENCY LIES IN YOUR PROFOUND UNDERSTANDING OF ONE OF THE FOLLOWING THREE SKILLS:

DISGUISE: YOU HAVE A FLAIR FOR MAKEUP AND STITCHING. YOU ARE ABLE TO QUICKLY CHANGE YOUR FACIAL APPEARANCE USING YOUR MAKEUP KIT, AND MAKE CHANGES TO YOUR APPAREL WITH WHAT YOU HAVE ON HAND USING YOUR SAVVY TAILORING SKILLS.

WEAPON THROWING: YOU POSSESS A MASTERY IN THE ART OF THROWING SMALL PROJECTILES, INCLUDING BUT NOT LIMITED TO KNIVES, HATCHETS, SHURIKENS, AND DARTS. YOUR BELT IS APPROPRIATELY LADEN WITH A VARIED AND DEADLY ARRAY OF SUCH PROJECTILES. THIS DEXTERITY ALSO AFFORDS YOU THE ABILITY TO MORE DEFTLY HANDLE A MANRIKI.

BURGLARY: YOU HAVE AN APTITUDE FOR PICKING ALL TYPES OF LOCKS. A SET OF LOCK PICKING TOOLS, IN YOUR HANDS, ARE MORE EFFECTIVE THAN A SKELETON KEY AND CROWBAR COMBINED. AS SUCH, YOU WILL BEGIN YOUR MISSION WITH THE AFOREMENTIONED TOOLS SO THAT YOU CAN DO WHAT YOU DO BEST.

CHOOSE ONE OF THE THREE ABOVE SPECIALTIES NOW

~~~~~~~~~~~~~~~~

YOUR PHYSICAL CONDITION IS REPRESENTED BY A NUMBER OF *LIFE* POINTS. THIS NUMBER DECREASES WHEN YOU ARE HIT OR ARE OTHERWISE INJURED. YOU MIGHT ALSO LOSE *LIFE* POINTS DUE TO ILLNESS, STARVATION, OR EXHAUSTION. *LIFE* POINTS CAN BE RESTORED WITH FIRST AID TREATMENT, A REMEDY, OR SOME OTHER MEANS OF REFRESHMENT.

IF YOU LOSE ALL OF YOUR *LIFE* POINTS AT ANY POINT DURING YOUR ADVENTURE, YOU HAVE DIED AND MUST IMMEDIATELY STOP READING. HOWEVER, THERE IS NOTHING STOPPING YOU FROM STARTING THE ADVENTURE OVER AGAIN! WHY NOT TRY IT WITH A DIFFERENT SPECIALTY?

THE AMOUNT OF TIME THAT HAS ELAPSED ON YOUR ADVENTURE IS OF PARTICULAR IMPORTANCE, AS YOU WILL OFTEN HAVE TO COMPLETE TASKS IN A SHORT SPAN OF TIME. SOMETIMES YOU WILL BE ASKED FOR THE CURRENT *TIME* VALUE, AS CERTAIN EVENTS WILL UNFOLD DIFFERENTLY DEPENDING ON THE AMOUNT OF *TIME* THAT HAS ELAPSED. EACH TIME YOU ENCOUNTER A *TIME* SYMBOL*, YOU WILL ADD 1 TO THE CURRENT *TIME* VALUE (WHICH BEGINS AT 0). REMEMBER THIS RULE EACH TIME YOU SEE THE FOLLOWING SYMBOL:

* TIME SYMBOL:

YOU BEGIN THIS MISSION WITH A PAIR OF BUTTERFLY KNIVES CONCEALED IN YOUR RIGHT SLEEVE. ALSO IN YOUR POSSESSION IS A CHAIN CONNECTING TWO SMALL, SPHERICAL WEIGHTS: A MANRIKI. IT IS QUITE EFFECTIVE AT HINDERING AN ENEMY'S ESCAPE -- WHETHER YOU USE IT TO ENTANGLE THEIR LEGS OR CONSTRICT THEIR NECK IS UP TO YOU.

A FOLDING BAMBOO LANTERN, SEVERAL CANDLES, AND A TINDER LIGHTER WILL ALLOW YOU TO BRAVE ANY PLACES SHROUDED IN DARKNESS.

DEPENDING ON YOUR CHOSEN SPECIALITY, YOU ALSO HAVE A MAKEUP KIT, A SELECTION OF THROWING WEAPONS, OR A TOOL KIT.

YOU ALSO POSSESS TWO VIALS OF POISON. ONE IS A POWDER AND MUST BE INGESTED BY THE VICTIM (THE *FEMME FATALE*); THE OTHER IS MORE VISCOUS, MAKING IT SUITABLE FOR THE COATING OF BLADES OR PROJECTILES (THE *BLACK LOTUS*). THE *FEMME FATALE* PROMISES A RAPID SEDATING EFFECT, WHILE THE *BLACK LOTUS* IS ONE THE OF THE MOST DEADLY SUBSTANCES FOUND ON EARTH. EACH VIAL CONTAINS THE EQUIVALENT OF ONE DOSE.

THE MASTER OF SERVANTS - THE HIGH PRIEST OF THE GODDESS NÜWA - HAS FURNISHED YOU WITH A *HEALTH POTION* TO AID YOU IN YOUR QUEST. YOU MAY DRINK IT AT ANY TIME, AND THE MIRACULOUS ELIXIR WILL IMMEDIATELY RESTORE *5 LIFE* POINTS, BUT YOU HAVE ONLY 3 DOSES FOR THE DURATION OF YOUR ADVENTURE. ANY POTIONS NOT USED EXPIRE AT THE END OF AN ADVENTURE.

NOTE THESE TWO VIALS OF POISON AND THE HEALTH POTION IN YOUR *INVENTORY*. THERE IS NO NEED, HOWEVER, TO NOTE THE REST OF YOUR STARTING EQUIPMENT. YOU WILL ALSO BE ABLE TO ADD CERTAIN OBJECTS TO YOUR *INVENTORY* THAT YOU FIND ALONG THE WAY, BUT ONLY WHERE THE TEXT INDICATES THAT YOU MAY DO SO.

FINALLY, YOU WILL SOMETIMES ENCOUNTER * AND # SYMBOLS DURING YOUR ADVENTURE. YOU MAY SAFELY IGNORE THESE SYMBOLS UNTIL SUCH TIME AS INSTRUCTIONS FOUND DURING YOUR ADVENTURE EXPLAIN THEIR MEANING.

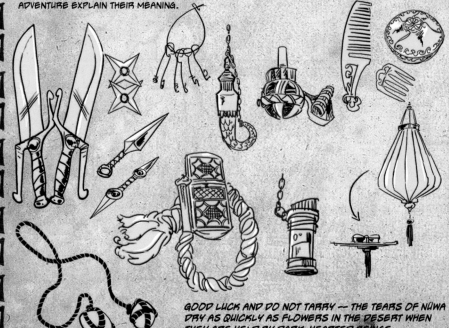

GOOD LUCK AND DO NOT TARRY -- THE TEARS OF NÜWA DRY AS QUICKLY AS FLOWERS IN THE DESERT WHEN THEY ARE HELD BY DARK-HEARTED BEINGS...

...IT IS HERE THAT THEY WERE STOLEN, IN THE ROOM OF INFINITE SPRING.

THE SIX TEARS OF *NÜWA*... THOSE SACRED SPROUTS HAVE BEEN KEPT IN THIS TEMPLE FOR CENTURIES NOW.

WE THOUGHT THEY WERE SAFE FROM SUCH MALICE!

THEY KILLED TWO COMBAT INSTRUCTORS, BROKE THROUGH THE DOOR, AND NEUTRALIZED THE PROTECTIVE GLYPH.

IT'S INCONCEIVABLE!

DID YOU RECOGNIZE THE THIEVES?

WELL...

FORTUNATELY, THE GODS DID NOT ABANDON US COMPLETELY: A MOON HUNTER SAW THEM FLEE FROM THE SCENE OF THE CRIME.

IT ALL HAPPENED AT DAWN. THERE WERE THREE ROBBERS, AND THEY'VE BEEN IDENTIFIED AS...

...TWO-HERON-MASANOKI...

...THE PYROMANIAC...

POW

... AND AE-CHA MENG, SORCERESS OF THE GARNET MOUNTAINS.

EACH HAS STOLEN TWO SPROUTS. PERHAPS THEIR NAMES MEAN SOMETHING TO YOU...

YOU MUST RETRIEVE THEM *WITHOUT DELAY!* THE SACRED SPROUTS WILL DECAY VERY QUICKLY OUTSIDE OF THE DIVINE POND. NÜWA WILL ABANDON US!

A THOUSAND CELESTIAL PLAGUES WILL DESCEND UPON THIS ENTIRE REGION IF THE SPROUTS ARE NOT RETURNED SOON!

OH, IT WILL BE FINE...

I KNOW THE LEGEND.

BLASPHEMER! THIS IS NO MERE LEGEND!

AND WHY DID YOU CALL ME?

YOU COULD HAVE ALREADY CLOSED THE CITY GATES AND SENT YOUR GUARDS TO DO YOUR BIDDING, NO? THEY COULD BE COMBING THE COUNTRYSIDE BY NOW.

THIS MIGHT SEEM STRANGE, BUT THE WITNESS SAW THE THIEVES GO SEPARATE WAYS AFTER LEAVING THE TEMPLE. THEY ARE, NO DOUBT, HIDING UNTIL THE DUST SETTLES, RATHER THAN BE CAUGHT RED HANDED OUT IN THE OPEN...

...ESPECIALLY IF THEY DON'T REALIZE THAT THEY'VE BEEN SPOTTED...

DISCRETION IS OF THE UTMOST IMPORTANCE. IF WE SOUND THE ALARM, THE CRIMINALS WILL DISAPPEAR AND LIKELY NEVER BE FOUND...

...AND, AS VICE-PREFECT, I MUST PREVENT THE ONSET OF PANIC. CHAOS WOULD SEIZE THE CITY IF THIS NEWS WERE TO SPREAD.

AND YOU CERTAINLY DON'T WANT THE HEAD PREFECT FINDING OUT. WHEN HE FINDS OUT, IT'S HIS RIGHT HAND THAT WILL SUFFER!

I UNDERSTAND...

...AND WHAT OF THE MOON HUNTER THAT SAW THEM?

LET'S JUST SAY, HE WON'T BE SPEAKING TO ANYONE.

YOU WILL BE REWARDED THREE HUNDRED COINS FOR EACH SPROUT RETURNED IN ONE PIECE, AND FIVE HUNDRED FOR THE CAPTURE OF EACH THIEF... OR THEIR HEAD.

DEAD OR ALIVE, IT'S NO MATTER. THEIR MISDEEDS LIVE ON.

RECOVER ALL THE SPROUTS, IF POSSIBLE... AND RETURN THEM **BEFORE THE SUN SETS!** IF YOU DO NOT, THE STARS OF THE NIGHT SKY WILL WITHER THE TEARS OF THE GODDESS! SHOULD THIS COME TO PASS, NOTHING WILL SAVE US FROM HER WRATH...

...NOTHING.

ONE THOUSAND COINS PER THIEF.

I'LL TAKE FIVE HUNDRED FOR THE SORCERESS...

?

IN YOUR MIND, AE-CHE MENG IS LESS DANGEROUS THAN THE OTHERS?

NO. JUST AN OLD SCORE TO SETTLE.

MIXING BUSINESS WITH PLEASURE. HARD TO PUT A PRICE ON THAT.

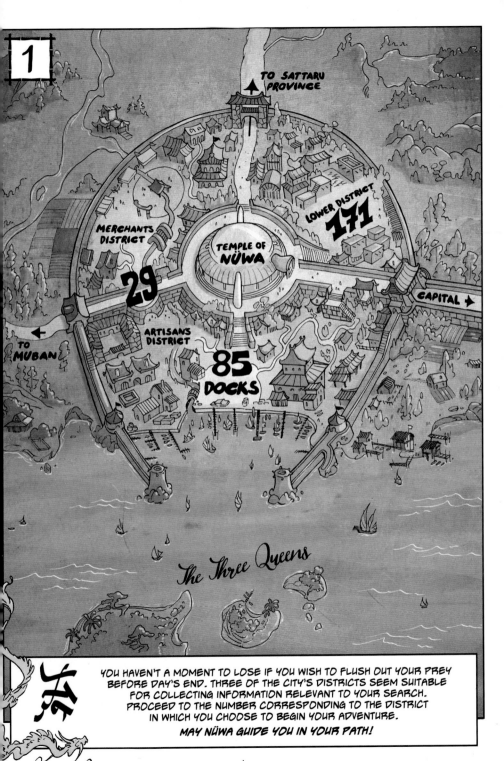

YOU HAVEN'T A MOMENT TO LOSE IF YOU WISH TO FLUSH OUT YOUR PREY BEFORE DAY'S END. THREE OF THE CITY'S DISTRICTS SEEM SUITABLE FOR COLLECTING INFORMATION RELEVANT TO YOUR SEARCH. PROCEED TO THE NUMBER CORRESPONDING TO THE DISTRICT IN WHICH YOU CHOOSE TO BEGIN YOUR ADVENTURE.

MAY NÜWA GUIDE YOU IN YOUR PATH!

2

IT WOULD NOT BE USEFUL TO THROW THE MANRIKI. THE MOUNT IS ALREADY TOO FAR AWAY. A DREADFUL PREMONITION TAKES HOLD OF YOU AS YOU RUSH TOWARDS THE CITY OF MUBAN AT *72*.

3

YOU'RE SAFE NOW, BUT YOU'D BEST KEEP MOVING...

4

APOLOGIES FOR SUCH AN UNCEREMONIOUS DEATH...

SUDDENLY YOU HEAR SOMEONE ELSE APPROACHING! GO TO *145* TO HIDE IN THE TALL GRASS OR TO *76* TO CROUCH DOWN & LEAVE THE AREA.

5

HOW DOES THIS SUIT YOU?

INCREDIBLE...

...AND BEEF GLUE, NO LESS!

REMOVE THE *ANIMAL GLUE* FROM YOUR *INVENTORY*, THEN GO TO *51*.

SHE GIVES YOU INFORMATION ON MASANOKI! HER SON WAS ON DUTY AT THE GATE OF PLENTY – WEST OF THE CITY – AND HE SAW THE FAMOUS WARRIOR PASS BY LAST NIGHT. THE GUARD SEEMED RATHER TERRIFIED, AND DIDN'T SEEM COMFORTABLE SHARING ANYTHING MORE.

ONCE YOU REACH *17*, IF NOTHING THERE INTERESTS YOU, YOU MAY TAKE AN IMMEDIATE SHORTCUT TO THE WEST GATE AT *34*. OR YOU COULD GO VISIT THE JEWELER AT *66* IF YOU PREFER.

THE PATH ON THE LEFT LEADS TO AN ABANDONED CRYPT, WHERE YOU MAY GAIN A GOOD VIEW OF THE SURROUNDING AREA. HOWEVER, THERE IS MUCH TO ACCOMPLISH, AND THE SUN REMINDS YOU THAT THE DAY IS PASSING QUICKER THAN YOU WOULD LIKE.

8

LEAVE ME ALONE!

HEY!

I OVERHEARD YOU. I KNOW WHERE ONE OF THEM IS!

FOLLOW ME...

GO TO *26* TO FOLLOW THE STRANGER, OR IGNORE HIM AND GO TO *46*.

9

REMOVE THE *SMOKE BOMB* FROM YOUR *INVENTORY*.

FIRE!

THERE IS NOTHING LEFT TO DO BUT AWAIT HIS RETURN AT *68*...

YOU CAN RUN AWAY TO **54** OR BRAVE THE ENCOUNTER AT **22**.

YOU CAN EXPLORE THIS SECRET PASSAGE TO **52** OR CONTINUE YOUR CLIMB TO **38**.

PERHAPS THIS PRECAUTION WAS UNNECESSARY... YOU INSPECT MUBAN WITHOUT INCIDENT AND QUICKLY FIND WHERE YOUR PREY IS HIDDEN. GO TO **55**.

13

AH YES, I KNOW OF WHAT YOU SPEAK!

BUT LET US GO OUT BACK, WHERE IT'S COOLER.

THE MAN IS RATHER CHATTY AND IT TAKES HIM A WHILE TO GET TO THE POINT: HE SAW MASANOKI HEAD FOR THE GATE OF PLENTY, TO LEAVE THE CITY, NO DOUBT. YOU LEAVE IMMEDIATELY TO **34**.

14

?!

AAAH!

YOU LOSE 4 LIFE # POINTS.

THAT WAS A CLOSE ONE... GO TO **50**.

15

16

LOOKS LIKE THIS ONE HAS A LONG RANGE WEAPON.
YOU'LL HAVE TO NEUTRALIZE HIM WITH YOUR MANRIKI,
BUT YOU ONLY GET ONE ATTEMPT...

GO TO *70* TO WAIT A LITTLE LONGER
OR TO *126* TO TREAD CLOSER
UNDER THE COVER OF THE TREES.

17

18

REMOVE THE *BLACK LOTUS* FROM YOUR *INVENTORY*, THEN PROCEED THROUGH THE WINDOW TO COMPLETE YOUR SINISTER TASK AT *73*.

19

THAT ISN'T GLUE OVER THERE?

I KNEW I HAD ONE LEFT! NÜWA BE PRAISED, YOU'VE SAVED MY LIFE!

GO TO *51*.

20

THIS WON'T BE MUCH OF A BURDEN, AND MAY EVEN PROVE USEFUL. ADD THE *ROPE* TO YOUR *INVENTORY*. THEN HEAD BACK TOWARDS MUBAN VIA *74*.

21

TOO BAD FOR THE SPROUTS THAT BRUTE WAS GUARDING, BUT MAKING USE OF THE DAYLIGHT YOU HAVE LEFT SEEMS LIKE A REASONABLE OPTION. RETURN TO THE CITY AT *100*.

22

YOU LOSE *6* LIFE POINTS. ESCAPE TO *54* WHILE YOU CAN.

23

YOU WOULD DO BEST TO PRACTICE CAUTION UP AHEAD. GO TO *12* IF YOU HAVE THE *DISGUISE* SPECIALTY.

THE POISON TAKES EFFECT QUICKLY, HAVING A NEAR IMMEDIATE EFFECT ON THE WARRIOR'S REFLEXES. HIS COUNTERATTACK COSTS YOU 3 *LIFE* POINTS *. GO TO 35.

HEY THERE CUTIE!

?!

I'M SUCH AN IDIOT...

POW!!

YOU LOSE 5 LIFE POINTS.

URG!

REUUUH! KOF KOF!

46

YOU CALL FOR ASSISTANCE, BUT NO ONE SEEMS TO BE HERE. WHOEVER OWNS THIS SHOP MUST BE VERY TRUSTING TO LEAVE IT UNATTENDED LIKE THIS...

28

HORSES! MASANOKI IS DEFINITELY IN THAT BUILDING. YOU RUSH TO 55 WITHOUT DELAY, AS THE DETONATION MAY HAVE ALERTED HIM.

TCHAK TCHAK

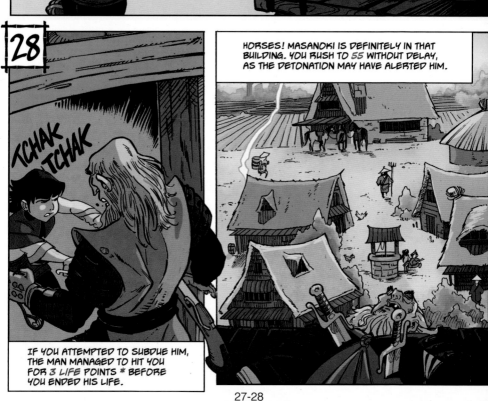

IF YOU ATTEMPTED TO SUBDUE HIM, THE MAN MANAGED TO HIT YOU FOR 3 *LIFE* POINTS * BEFORE YOU ENDED HIS LIFE.

29

THIS AREA OF THE CITY HAS FEW (IF ANY) SECRETS TO TELL YOU. THE PATH TO THE LEFT HEADS TO THE GATE OF PLENTY VIA THE ARTISANS' DISTRICT. THE PATH ON THE RIGHT WILL TAKE YOU THE MERCHANTS' DISTRICT.

30

HEURK

A MASTERFUL SHOT THAT SILENTLY AND INSTANTLY ELIMINATES THE BODYGUARD. IT'S TIME TO FLUSH THE SCOUNDREL OUT OF HIDING... GO TO 137.

31

SORRY, THAT DOESN'T MEAN ANYTHING TO ME. TRY TALKING TO U-THANT, THE GLASS BLOWER. HE'S A BIT OF A CHATTERBOX, BUT HE KNOWS EVERYTHING THAT GOES ON IN THE DISTRICT.

GO TO 46 TO FOLLOW HER ADVICE OR TO 37 IF YOU'D PREFER TO QUESTION THE CARPENTER.

32

BY DESCENDING THE STAIRCASE, YOU WILL LEAVE THE BARRACKS AND THE CITY BEHIND TO HEAD FOR MUBAN.

33

IF POISON SEEMS APPROPRIATE, GO TO 57 TO USE THE *FEMME FATALE*, OR 18 TO USE THE *BLACK LOTUS*. IF NOT, YOU CAN SNEAK IN SURREPTITIOUSLY TO 73.

34

35

YOU BARELY HAVE THE TIME TO SAVOUR THIS VICTORY BEFORE BEING ALERTED BY A WHINNY OUTSIDE. TAKE THE SPROUTS AND SEE WHAT'S GOING ON AT *BO*.

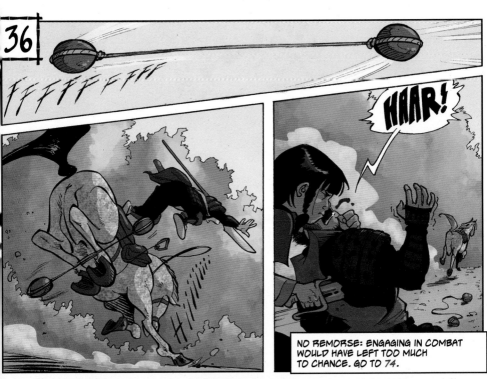

NO REMORSE: ENGAGING IN COMBAT WOULD HAVE LEFT TOO MUCH TO CHANCE. GO TO *74*.

NOT OFF TO A GREAT START... IF YOU HAVE THE *ANIMAL GLUE*, GO TO *5*. OTHERWISE, VISIT THE OPPOSITE WORKSHOP AT *56* OR CONTINUE DOWN THE ROAD TO *46*.

38

SOLDIERS ONLY! YOU'RE GOING TO HAVE TO SPEAK TO SERGEANT TSAKAGYN.

YOU'RE NOT HERE TO CAUSE A RUCKUS. GO BACK DOWN TO 32.

39

A GARUDA!

IT IS SAID THAT THIS GUARDIAN SPIRIT REPELS DEMONS AND PUNISHES THOSE WITH BAD INTENTIONS. IF YOU TAKE IT, GO TO 67. IF YOU'D PREFER NOT TO, GO TO 46.

40

SMART THINKING! LAUNCH A COUNTERATTACK AT 235.

41

YEAH, WE SAW MASANOKI PASS BY THIS MORNING. NOT THE OTHER TWO, THOUGH.

AOW!

LOSE *5* *LIFE* POINTS #.

GO TO *77* TO TAKE REFUGE BEHIND A BUILDING, OR TO *64* TO CHARGE TOWARDS THE MILL'S ENTRANCE, OR TO *21* TO FLEE THE VILLAGE.

44

GO TO *24* IF YOU HAVE THE *DISGUISE* SPECIALTY. OTHERWISE, GO TO *38*.

45

??!

YYYAAAAH!

GO TO *36* IF YOU HAVE THE *WEAPON THROWING* SPECIALTY. OTHERWISE GO TO *2*.

46

47

THIS VIOLENT, INSTINCTIVE BLOW COMES AT A PRICE: LOSE *2 LIFE POINTS*. IF YOU DON'T SUCCUMB TO SHOCK, GO TO *112* TO FINISH THE JOB.

48

A QUICK, BUT METHODIC SEARCH UNVEILS AN ENCHANTED DOJO.

ADD THE *PARRYING NECKLACE* TO YOUR *INVENTORY*. FROM NOW ON, EACH *LIFE POINT* LOSS INFLICTED BY TEXT WITH THE * SYMBOL IS REDUCED BY 1. ALTHOUGH IT'S UNLIKELY ANYONE WILL NOTICE THE ITEM IS MISSING, YOU'D PREFER TO LEAVE FOR MUBAN SOONER RATHER THAN LATER. GO TO 71.

49

THE GUARD SEEMS STUNNED AS YOU ENTER THE ROOM.

WASTING NO TIME, YOU INTERROGATE HIM ABOUT MASANOKI WITHOUT SHARING TOO MUCH ABOUT YOUR MISSION.

HE LEFT THE CITY THIS MORNING, AT DAWN. I OVERHEARD THAT HE'D BE STAYING IN MUBAN, BUT THAT'S ALL I KNOW.

IF YOU HAVE THE *LINGLING-O*, YOU CAN OFFER IT TO MAKE HIM TALK A LITTLE MORE AT 63. IF NOT, RETURN TO 32.

50

51

THE CARPENTER DIDN'T SEE ANY THIEVES. HOWEVER, HE TELLS YOU THAT A DIGNITARY FROM SATTARA ARRIVED IN MUBAN YESTERDAY, WHERE HE IS STAYING INCOGNITO. THIS IS NO COINCIDENCE.

LEAVE THE WORKSHOP AND GO TO 46. ONCE THERE, IF NOTHING INTERESTS YOU, YOU MAY TAKE AN IMMEDIATE SHORTCUT TO THE WEST GATE AT 34.

52

THE ROOM LOOKS EMPTY, BUT BE ON YOUR GUARD. ENTER TO 48.

53

HIS KNEE CONNECTS WITH YOUR ABDOMEN AND YOU LOSE 3 LIFE POINTS. YOU CAN GRAB HOLD AND ROLL HIM INTO THE BUSH AT 65, OR KICK HIM IN THE HEAD AT 47.

54

A RAHUJI! WHAT'S WITH THIS CRAZY FAMILY?

55

MASANOKI!

IF YOU HAVE A *SMOKE BOMB*, YOU CAN USE IT TO CREATE A DIVERSION AND GO TO 9. TO EXECUTE A DIFFERENT MANEUVER, GO TO 33.

56

YOU WAIT A SHORT WHILE FOR THE DRUG TO TAKE EFFECT BEFORE MAKING YOUR MOVE AT *25*.

REMOVE THE *FEMME FATALE* FROM YOUR *INVENTORY*.

IF YOU DON'T WANT TO BUY ANYTHING, MAKE ROOM FOR OTHER CUSTOMERS.

PRESSING HER WITH FURTHER QUESTIONS SEEMS FUTILE, ESPECIALLY AS THE AREA BECOMES MORE CROWDED. YOU CAN LET YOURSELF BE CARRIED BY THE SEA OF PEOPLE TO *17*, OR PUSH THROUGH THE CROWD TO A NEIGHBORING AREA VIA *66*.

59 IF YOU HAVE THE *BURGLARY* SPECIALTY, GO TO *61* TO TAKE THE OBJECT AND DISAPPEAR INTO THE CROWD.

OTHERWISE, YOU CAN CONTINUE ON TO *17* OR TRY TO MAKE YOUR WAY TO THE NEAREST STALL AT *66*.

60

PAW!

AARH!

YOU LOSE *9 LIFE* POINTS #! IF YOU'RE STILL DRAWING BREATH, GET UP AND HIDE BEHIND A NEARBY HOUSE AT *77*, OR FLEE THE CITY TO *21*.

61 THE RISK WAS WORTH THE REWARD. THE *LINGLING-O* ARE SOME OF THE MOST PRIZED JEWELRY AT THE MOMENT. *INVENTORY* AND DEPART FOR *17*.

62 SNEAK INSIDE TO *32*.

63

REMOVE THE *LINGLING-O* FROM YOUR *INVENTORY*. IN RETURN FOR YOUR GENEROSITY, HE TELLS YOU THAT HE CROSSED PATHS WITH THE FAMOUS WARRIOR LAST NIGHT. DESPITE HIS FEAR OF REPRISAL, HE ALSO SHARES WITH YOU...

...THAT THE WARRIOR LIVES NEAR THE BLACKSMITH. OTHERS HAVE JOINED HIM IN MUBAN: ONE IS STATIONED AT THE CRYPT IN THE WOODS TO WATCH THE ROAD, WHILE THE OTHER IS IN THE MILL.

ARMED WITH THIS VALUABLE NEW INFORMATION, HEAD TO MUBAN AT *71*.

64

!!!

DECIDE WHETHER YOU WILL ATTACK TO KILL OR SIMPLY TO SUBDUE HIM BEFORE HEADING TO *28*.

65

DIRTY...
LITTLE...

ALL HE HAS LEFT ARE INSULTS AS YOUR BLADE SINKS INTO HIM. GO TO 112.

66

TAKING ADVANTAGE OF THE CROWDED MASS, A THIEF LIFTS ONE OF YOUR BELONGINGS. REMOVE AN ITEM OF YOUR CHOICE FROM YOUR *INVENTORY*. GO TO *58* TO SPEAK WITH THE JEWELLER, OR TO *6* TO SPEAK WITH THE GARDENER.

67

YOU SUDDENLY FEEL WEAK AND NAUSEOUS AFTER TOUCHING THE STATUETTE, BUT THE SENSATION LASTS ONLY A MOMENT. YOU LOSE *2 LIFE* POINTS. ADD THE *GARUDA* TO YOUR *INVENTORY* AND HEAD TO *46*.

68

YOU TAKE CARE TO MAKE CERTAIN YOUR FIRST STRIKE PROVES FATAL. OTHERWISE, THINGS COULD GET MESSY.

GO TO *35*.

69

?!

IF YOU HAVE THE *WEAPON THROWING* SPECIALTY, PROCEED TO *36*. OTHERWISE, GO TO *2*.

70

FFFFFFF

THE BODYGUARD DRAWS CLOSER TO YOU, UNAWARE OF YOUR PRESENCE. YOU WAIT FOR THE RIGHT MOMENT AND THROW THE MANRIKI. GO TO *30*.

71

72

JUST AS YOU FEARED, THE HERON HAS FLOWN THE COOP. MASANOKI LEFT THE CITY BY HORSE, SO CATCHING UP WITH HIM IS UNLIKELY. HEAD BACK TO THE CITY AT *100*.

73 CRAK

GO TO *25* IF YOU'VE JUST LACED YOUR BLADES WITH *BLACK LOTUS*. OTHERWISE, GO TO *79*.

74

THAT LOOKOUT WAS DEFINITELY LINKED TO TWO-HERON-MASANOKI. YOU ARE NOW CERTAIN THAT THE BRUTE HAS HIDDEN HIMSELF IN THE CITY...

75

YOU CAN BYPASS HIM AND TRY TO TAKE HIM BY SURPRISE AT *14*, OR MAKE YOUR PRESENCE KNOWN AT *45*.

76

YOU LOSE *3 LIFE* POINTS ✳ BEFORE YOU CAN RETALIATE. IF YOU'RE STILL ALIVE, GO TO *109*.

?!!

THE BLADE PLUMMETS INTO YOU AND TEARS APART YOUR INSIDES. THE WARRIOR'S DEMONIC LAUGH IS THE LAST SOUND YOU EVER HEAR. SO ENDS YOUR MISSION...

NO ONE HAS EVER BESTED HIM IN SINGLE COMBAT. HAVING WOUNDED HIM AT ALL IS YOUR ONLY CONSOLATION AS YOU EXHALE YOUR LAST BREATH...

80 A MYSTERIOUS SUSPECT TAKES OFF DOWN A ROAD LEADING TO SATTARU. BUT BECAUSE THAT DESPICABLE SCOUNDREL CUT THE HOCKS OF THE REMAINING HORSES, YOU HAVE NO WAY TO FOLLOW HIM.

NO MATTER. ADD *TWO SPROUTS* TO YOUR *INVENTORY* AND MAKE YOUR WAY BACK TO THE CITY AT *100*.

81 IF YOU HAVE BEEN TOLD OF THE FLOWER BOAT AND WISH TO VISIT IT, YOU MAY GO TO *142*.

82

YOU DON'T SEE LUCILLE, THE OWNER OF THIS ESTABLISHMENT. IF YOU HAVE THE **DISGUISE** SPECIALTY, YOU MAY PROCEED TO *98*.

83

YOU MUST QUICKLY FIND THE SORCERER'S HIDING PLACE TO MAKE UP FOR THE TIME YOU LOST WHILE CROSSING. IF LUCILLE TOLD YOU ABOUT THE SECRET ENTRANCE, YOU MAY GO THERE NOW BY ADDING THE NUMBER SHE GAVE YOU TO THE CURRENT PARAGRAPH.

BETTER NOT TAKE ANY RISK.
BEST NOT MISS THE TARGET.

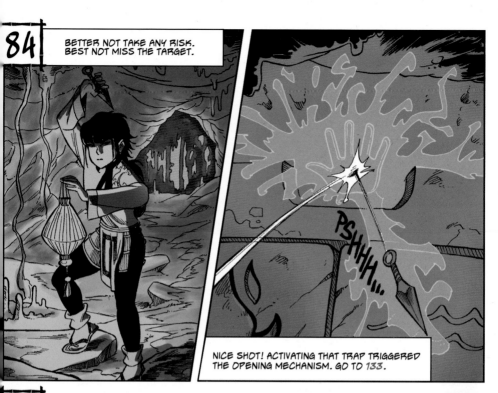

NICE SHOT! ACTIVATING THAT TRAP TRIGGERED
THE OPENING MECHANISM. GO TO *133*.

THE TWO PATHS BOTH LEAD TO THE HARBOR. THE ONE
ON THE RIGHT PASSES THROUGH A RATHER NOTORIOUS
DISTRICT. THERE'S NO GUARANTEE THAT WITNESSES
YOU FIND IN THAT DIRECTION WILL BE CO-OPERATIVE.

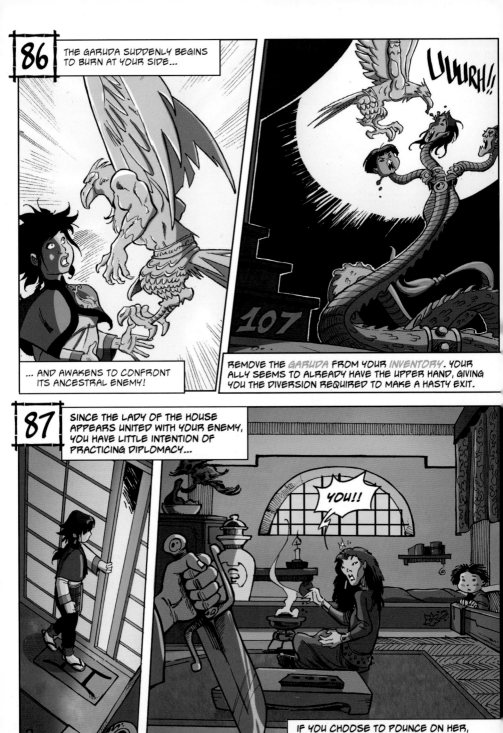

86 THE GARUDA SUDDENLY BEGINS TO BURN AT YOUR SIDE...

UUURH!!

107

... AND AWAKENS TO CONFRONT ITS ANCESTRAL ENEMY!

REMOVE THE *GARUDA* FROM YOUR *INVENTORY*. YOUR ALLY SEEMS TO ALREADY HAVE THE UPPER HAND, GIVING YOU THE DIVERSION REQUIRED TO MAKE A HASTY EXIT.

87 SINCE THE LADY OF THE HOUSE APPEARS UNITED WITH YOUR ENEMY, YOU HAVE LITTLE INTENTION OF PRACTICING DIPLOMACY...

YOU!!

IF YOU CHOOSE TO POUNCE ON HER, GO TO *148*. OR YOU COULD GRAB THE CHILD AT *132*.

HIIIIIIIIIIII,,,

CLAC,,

HEY! THE HORSES!!

THAT'LL KEEP THEM BUSY LONG ENOUGH TO LET YOU MAKE A GETAWAY. HEAD TO *16*.

THESE PLEASANTRIES HAVE GONE ON LONG ENOUGH! THIS CROOK HAS NOTHING TO TEACH YOU ABOUT THE THREE THIEVES. ALL HE SEES IS A POTENTIAL CUSTOMER. YOU CAN VISIT THE SHOP ACROSS THE WAY AT *135* OR HEAD DIRECTLY TO THE HARBOR AT *81*.

WE'RE NOT ACCEPTING NEW GIRLS! GET OUT OF HERE!

BEST TO DO AS YOU'RE TOLD NOW THAT YOU'VE BEEN SPOTTED. HEAD TO *81*. YOU WON'T BE WELCOME HERE ANYMORE.

91

THEIR BREAK WON'T LAST LONG. YOU CAN SNEAK CLOSER BENEATH THE COVER OF THE TREES TO *149* OR FOLLOW THE RIVER BANK TO HEAD DIRECTLY TO THE PALANQUIN AT *122*.

92

WELL, WELL! WHAT CAN I HELP YOU WITH, CUTIE?

YOU CAN PLAY ALONG AT *144* OR INTERROGATE HIM MORE CAUTIOUSLY AT *129*.

93

LUCILLE CERTAINLY DIDN'T LIE ABOUT THE LOCATION OF THE TUNNEL. IT SHOULD LEAD TO AE-CHA'S LAIR... ...OR IT COULD BE A TRAP.

94

IF YOU SPOKE WITH THE FISHER, GO TO *110*. OTHERWISE, RETURN TO *81*.

95

THE METALLIC MARBLE CONNECTS AND YOU LOSE *5 LIFE* POINTS #. BUT YOU CLENCH YOUR TEETH AND STRIKE BACK AT *30*.

96

GOT HER! LET'S TAKE HER INSIDE!

AAARH ?!!

A PUNCH IN YOUR BACK AND A HEADLOCK COST YOU *3 LIFE* POINTS. BUT YOU WON'T BE TAKEN ANYWHERE BY THIS LECHEROUS OLD FOOL. SHOW HIM WHO'S BOSS AT *118*.

97

A FLASH OF INTENSE HATRED, SUDDEN AND IRRATIONAL, FOCUSES YOUR ATTENTION ON THE ONE WHO ROBBED YOU OF YOUR FORMER COMPANION. TO THROW YOUR MANRIKI, GO TO *140*. OR, TRY TO SNEAK BEHIND HER AT *117*.

98 TAKING ONE OF THE COURTESAN'S DIADEMS WAS CHILD'S PLAY...

... AND JUST AS YOU HOPED, YOUR NEW LOOK OPENS THE DOOR FOR YOU! GO TO *155*.

99

YOU ARE FAR TOO FAMILIAR WITH THE ART OF POISON TO BE CAUGHT DRINKING UNKNOWN ELIXIRS. ESPECIALLY IF THEY WERE CONCOCTED BY AE-CHA, THAT MINX... RETURN TO *133* AND KEEP LOOKING FOR HER.

100 IF YOUR CURRENT *TIME* VALUE IS *11* OR GREATER, GO TO *200*. OTHERWISE RETURN TO *1* AND CHOOSE ANOTHER DISTRICT.

101

YOU LOSE *4 LIFE* POINTS *
BEFORE RESPONDING AT *235*.

102

DEBRIS FROM THE BOAT FLIES AT YOUR FACE
AND THERE'S NOTHING YOU CAN DO TO AVOID IT.
LOSE *5 LIFE* POINTS AND GO TO *164*.

103

WHAT A RACKET! MAKING YOURSELF HEARD WON'T BE EASY...

105 YOU LOSE *2 LIFE* POINTS SCRAPING UP AGAINST A POISONOUS SUMAC BUSH.

BUT SEEING THE TOWER REINVIGORATES YOU: AE-CHA MENG IS HERE, YOU'RE SURE OF IT!

106

CURSE YOU! GET OUT OF THERE!

DO AS YOUR TOLD AND HEAD TO *136* OR ROW AWAY TO *152.*

107 AH, A MAGIC TRAP! IF YOU HAVE THE *ROCK SALT*, GO TO 151. OTHERWISE, DETERMINE WHICH THREE SYMBOLS BELONG IN THE LAST COLUMN AND GO TO *124.*

THAT WAS TOO CLOSE FOR COMFORT. HE ALMOST HAD YOU. GO TO *16*.

??!

A SEA MONSTER! IF YOU HAVE A *FLUTE*, GO TO *165*. OTHERWISE, YOU CAN ATTEMPT TO RAM THE BEAST AT *102* OR STAY STILL FOR THE MOMENT AT *146*.

111

YOU LOSE *7 LIFE* POINTS. IF YOU MANAGED TO LIVE THROUGH THE BLAST, YOU EXPERIENCE THE BITTER RELIEF THAT TRIGGERING THE TRAP ALSO OPENED THE PASSAGE. HEAD THROUGH THE TUNNEL TO *133*.

112

113

EMPTYING THE POISON INTO THAT ALCOHOL WAS CHILD'S PLAY. REMOVE THE *FEMME FATALE* FROM YOUR *INVENTORY* AND ADD THE *FLUTE* IN ITS PLACE. HEAD TO THE HARBOR AT *81*.

114

IMPRESSIVE FIND! ADD THIS *DEFENSIVE AMULET* TO YOUR *INVENTORY*. FROM NOW ON, EACH *LIFE* POINT LOSS INFLICTED BY TEXT WITH THE # SYMBOL IS REDUCED BY *2*. RETURN TO *133*.

115

NO ENTRY ALLOWED. PRIVATE AREA!

GO TO *123* TO SAY: "I MUST SPEAK TO LUCILLE: BY ORDER OF THE VICE-PREFECT!"

OR GO TO *90* TO SAY: "I'M THE NEW..."

116

TAH

AOW!

A BLOW FROM HIS NUNCHUCKS MAKES YOU LOSE *2 LIFE* POINTS ✱. YOU CAN GRAB HOLD AND ROLL HIM INTO THE BUSH AT *65*, OR KICK HIM IN THE HEAD AT *47*.

117

?!

SHE SLIPS FROM YOUR GRASP AND ESCAPES WITH THE SPROUTS! THIS ENTIRE TRIP WAS A WASTE. GO TO *159*.

118

WILL YOU FIND REFUGE IN THE TAVERN AT *103* OR HEAD FOR THE HARBOR AT *81*?

119

THE SYMBOL OF THE SHADOW GUILD IS WELL KNOWN IN THE LOWER DISTRICT. THIS COULD PROVE USEFUL. ADD THE *STARFISH* TO YOUR *INVENTORY* AND HEAD TO *115* TO EXPLORE THE GROUND FLOOR.

120

THE SAILORS COME FROM PEITAI HARBOR, FAR WEST OF HERE. THEY'VE NEVER HEARD OF THE 3 ROGUES YOU SPEAK OF. RETURN TO *81*.

121

AH, A UNIQUE OBJECT AMONGST THE FORGOTTEN TRASH. YOU MAY ADD THE *FUMIGANT* TO YOUR *INVENTORY* BEFORE YOU RETURN TO *138*.

122

I CAN'T HOLD IT ANYMORE, YOURI. GONNA GO DRAIN THE LIZARD.

YOU CAN TAKE ADVANTAGE OF THIS OPPORTUNITY TO ELIMINATE HIM AT *4* OR TRY TO SNEAK INTO THE PALANQUIN AT *157*.

123

OF COURSE, GO RIGHT IN.

THE FEAR OF AUTHORITY. ALWAYS EFFECTIVE WITH HIS SORT. GO TO *87*.

124

IF YOU DID NOT TRACE THESE SYMBOLS IN THIS ORDER, THE DOOR OPENS BUT THE LAYER OF CHALK SUDDENLY IGNITES. YOU LOSE *6 LIFE* POINTS.

125

THE VICE PREFECT WOULD NOT HAVE TOLERATED A COMPLETE FAILURE ON YOUR PART. STEALING A HORSE AND ABANDONING THE CITY WEIGHS HEAVY ON YOUR CONSCIENCE, BUT YOUR FUTURE LIES ELSEWHERE NOW, FAR FROM WEAPONS AND POISON. SUCH A LIFE NO LONGER SUITS YOU...

VISIT THE **TABLE OF ACHIEVMENTS** AT THE END OF THE BOOK TO CALCULATE YOUR FINAL SCORE.

126

WILL YOU THROW YOUR MANRIKI AT *70* OR STAY PERFECTLY STILL AT *95*?

127

YOU TAKE A WILD GUESS AT WHAT THIS FLOOR IS RESERVED FOR AND QUIETLY HEAD BACK DOWNSTAIRS TO NEGOTIATE WITH THE GUARD AT *115*.

128

A NAGA!!

GO TO *86* IF YOU HAVE A *GARUDA*. OTHERWISE, GO TO *162*.

129

DOESN'T MEAN ANYTHING TO ME. SORRY, BUT I HAVE WORK TO DO

YOU DO TOO. HEAD TO THE TAVERN AT *103* OR GO DIRECTLY TO THE HARBOR AT *81*.

130

YOU CAN KNOCK OUT THE GUARD AT *212* OR TAKE STAIRS AT *189*.

131

THE BURNING WIND REDUCES YOUR HEALTH BY *6 LIFE* POINTS. IF YOU'RE STILL ABLE, GO TO *117*.

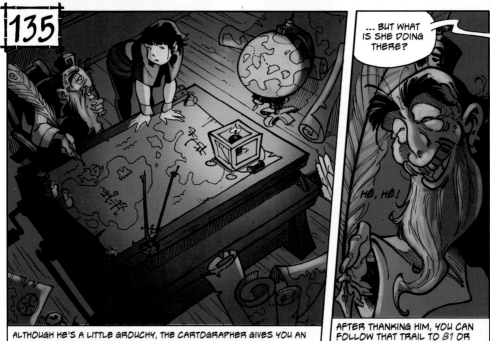

FISH! FISH FOR SALE! MY FISH ARE SO BEAUTIFUL!

YOU ARE FORCED TO ENDURE A SEEMINGLY ENDLESS REPRIMAND. YOU DO NOT FLINCH OR REPLY FOR FEAR THAT THE EXPERIENCE WILL ONLY LAST LONGER. HE FINALLY FINISHES HIS RANT AND YOU LEAVE FOR *81*.

YOU'VE FINALLY BOUNCED BACK: BUSINESS IS GOOD DURING HIGH TIDE!

HE LEAPS ON YOU FROM OUT OF NOWHERE. INSTINCTIVELY, YOU PROTECT YOUR LEFT SIDE AT *40* OR YOUR RIGHT AT *101*.

YOU CAN TAKE OUT YOUR BUTTERFLY KNIVES AT *131* OR GRAB HOLD OF HER AT *104*.

141

YOU THINK FOR A MOMENT AND DECIDE AGAINST SCALING THE TOWER. TAKE THE DOOR AT *163*...

142

143

REMOVE THE **BLACK LOTUS** FROM YOUR **INVENTORY**.

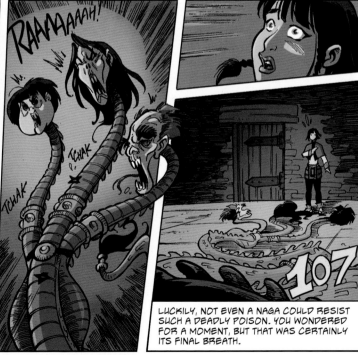

LUCKILY, NOT EVEN A NAGA COULD RESIST SUCH A DEADLY POISON. YOU WONDERED FOR A MOMENT, BUT THAT WAS CERTAINLY ITS FINAL BREATH.

144

THE SORCERESS YOU SPEAK OF. I THINK I KNOW WHERE SHE IS, BUT...

YES?

SUDDENLY, YOU NO LONGER FEEL SAFE. YOU CAN REACH FOR YOUR WEAPONS AT *96* OR TAKE YOUR LEAVE AT *118*.

145

RHAA

HA!

YOU LOSE *6 LIFE* POINTS * BEFORE COUNTERING THE ATTACK AT *109*. THAT IS, IF YOU'RE STILL ALIVE.

146

FAILING TO NOTICE YOUR PRESENCE, THE MASSIVE SEA CREATURE PLOWS THROUGH YOU, KNOCKING YOU FROM YOUR VESSEL. YOU LOSE *2 LIFE* POINTS AND RESURFACE AT *164*.

147

IT TOOK A FEW MORE ROUNDS BEFORE HE WOULD LET GO OF IT. ADD THE *FLUTE* TO YOUR *INVENTORY*, THEN HEAD FOR THE HARBOR AT *81*.

148

SHE SUBMITS QUICKLY AND YOU LEARN THAT AE-CHA MENG CAN BE FOUND ON THE LARGEST OF *THE THREE QUEENS*, IN A DISUSED TOWER AT THE HEART OF THE ISLAND.

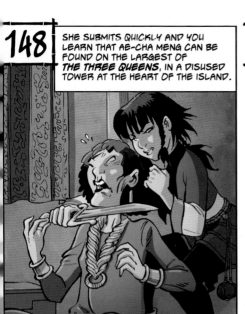

YOU DECIDE TO TAKE THE WOMAN'S BOAT, WHICH IS TIED OUT BEHIND THE BUILDING. IT ISN'T LONG BEFORE YOU HOP IN AND START PADDLING. GO TO *110*.

149

I CAN'T HOLD IT ANYMORE, YOUBI. GONNA GO DRAIN THE LIZARD.

YOU CAN TAKE ADVANTAGE OF THIS OPPORTUNITY TO ELIMINATE HIM AT *4*. BUT IF YOU HAVE THE *BURGLARY* SPECIALTY, YOU CAN PICK THE LOCK SECURING THEIR HORSES AND SCARE THEM OFF AT *88*.

150

EVEN THOUGH THE FUTURE OF THE CITY IS IN DOUBT, YOU RECEIVE YOUR REWARD (CONSULT THE *INTRODUCTION* TO DETERMINE THE EXACT AMOUNT), FOR THE VICE-PREFECT IS A MAN OF HIS WORD.

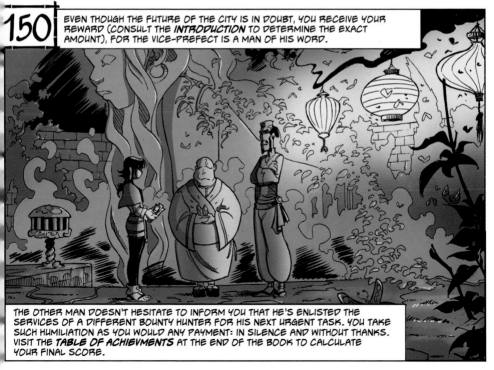

THE OTHER MAN DOESN'T HESITATE TO INFORM YOU THAT HE'S ENLISTED THE SERVICES OF A DIFFERENT BOUNTY HUNTER FOR HIS NEXT URGENT TASK. YOU TAKE SUCH HUMILIATION AS YOU WOULD ANY PAYMENT: IN SILENCE AND WITHOUT THANKS. VISIT THE *TABLE OF ACHIEVMENTS* AT THE END OF THE BOOK TO CALCULATE YOUR FINAL SCORE.

151

YOU CAN NOW SAFELY CROSS THE GLYPH TRACED BY THE MAGICIAN. REMOVE THE *ROCK SALT* FROM YOUR *INVENTORY*.

152

YOU LOSE *4 LIFE* POINTS. YOU CLENCH YOUR TEETH TO OVERCOME THE PAIN, AS YOU CAN'T STOP UNTIL YOU'RE SAFELY OUT OF REACH. GO TO *110*.

153

154

COME. WE CAN CHAT INSIDE.

HIS NONCHALANCE WORRIES YOU, AS TIME IS PRECIOUS. ALL THE SAME, YOU CAN STEP INSIDE AT *89*, OR HEAD TO THE SHOP ACROSS THE WAY AT *135*.

155

IT'S JUST THE TWO OF US NOW, LUCILLE!

STEP INTO 87.

156

YOU BREATHE A SIGH OF RELIEF BEFORE CONTINUING THROUGH THE TUNNEL TO *133*.

157

BLAAAAAREH

THERE'S SOMEONE HERE!

TOK

AWFULLY DIFFICULT TO GET UP AFTER BEING SHOT POINT BLANK BY A CROSSBOW, IN THE HEAD NO LESS...

158

THE INNKEEPER SEEMS FRIENDLY ENOUGH, BUT DOESN'T SEEM TO HAVE ANY INFORMATION RELEVANT TO YOUR MISSION. PLUS, THE SMOKE IS GETTING ON YOUR NERVES, SO YOU HEAD FOR THE HARBOR AND FRESH AIR AT *81*.

159

IT'S THE SECOND TIME NOW THAT YOU'VE USE A TELEPORTATION GLYPH, BUT YOU'RE JUST AS APPREHENSIVE AS YOU WERE THE FIRST TIME...

IN YOUR MIND, YOU VISUALIZE THE HEART OF THE CITY BEFORE BEING TRANSPORTED TO *100*.

160

THE FISHERMAN SAW AE-CHA-MENG AT DAYBREAK.

SHE WAS HEADED FOR THE LARGEST OF *THE THREE QUEENS*, IN A BOAT...

...CAPTAINED BY A MAN KNOWN TO WORK FOR LUCILLE, THE PROPRIETOR OF THE FLOWER BOAT. YOU CAN "BORROW" A BOAT AND HEAD TO *106* OR LOOK ELSEWHERE AT *81*.

161

THE NUMEROUS DETOURS AND SWARMS OF INSECTS WEAR ON YOU. LOSE *1 LIFE* POINT.

162

AAH!!

YOU ARE TORN LIMB FROM LIMB BY RAZOR SHARP FANGS. YOU HAVE FAILED YOUR MISSION. UNLIKE YOU, THE TOWER GUARDIAN HAS ACCOMPLISHED ITS GOAL...

163

IT SEEMS THAT AE-CHA HAS ENTRUSTED THIS LARGE REPTILE WITH GUARDING THE STAIRCASE! BEST NOT TO WAKE IT. HOWEVER, IF YOU STILL HAVE A DOSE OF *BLACK LOTUS* AND THE **WEAPON THROWING** SPECIALTY, YOU CAN ATTEMPT TO SLAY THE BEAST AT *143*.

164

FORTUNATELY, YOU CAN SEE THE SHORE, BUT YOU'RE EXHAUSTED BY THE TIME YOU FINALLY SET FOOT ON THE ISLAND AT *83*.

165

THE RESPLENDENT SOUNDS THAT FLOW FROM THE INSTRUMENT HAVE AN IMMEDIATE EFFECT AS YOU WATCH THE CREATURE PLUNGE BACK INTO THE DEPTHS.
YOU CONTINUE ON YOUR TRAVELS TO *83*.

166

AN INSECT BITES YOU, AND YOU GNASH YOUR TEETH TO KEEP YOURSELF FROM SCREAMING. THE VENOM IS NOT LETHAL, BUT ISN'T HARMLESS EITHER AND YOU LOSE *4 LIFE* POINTS. YOU CARRY ON AND REACH THE NEXT FLOOR AT *107*.

167

SORRY, SWEETHEART, BUT THIS SIMPLY WON'T DO. YOU'VE BECOME TOO DANGEROUS.

WAIT!

IT'S NO USE. SHOWING THE FAINTEST COMPASSION, HE SENDS ONE OF HIS ASSOCIATES TO COME DO THE DIRTY WORK. YOUR MISSION ENDS HERE.

168 YOU WALK THROUGH THE TUNNEL UNTIL YOU DISCOVER THAT YOUR PATH IS BLOCKED BY A RATHER CURIOUS OBSTACLE...

AT THE END OF TIME, ALL WILL BE BUT DUST, MUD, AND SMOKE.

YOU MUST TOUCH THREE STONES ON THE THIRD ROW BEFORE ACTIVATING THE MECHANISM. ONCE YOU HAVE MADE YOUR CHOICE, GIVE EACH COLUMN A NUMBER (FROM 1 TO 6, LEFT TO RIGHT) AND GO TO THE PARAGRAPH ASSOCIATED WITH THOSE NUMBERS. IF THE RESULT DOESN'T MAKE SENSE, GO TO *111*. YOU CAN TRY TO PASS THE OBSTACLE ANOTHER WAY AT *84* IF YOU HAVE THE **WEAPON THROWING** SPECIALTY...

169 BEFORE LONG, YOU LOOK LIKE AN OLD ROBBER FROM THE LOWER DISTRICT. AND, IF THE DISGUISE DOESN'T WORK, YOU CAN ALWAYS TAKE A MORE FORCEFUL APPROACH...

AH! IT'S YOU, SLU-TZI?

MMM...

NO PROBLEM. CONTINUE ON TO *176*.

170

FALLING THROUGH THE TRAPDOOR COSTS YOU *3 LIFE* POINTS. IF YOU HAVE THE *ROPE*, YOU CAN FASHION A CRUDE GRAPPLING HOOK TO CLIMB BACK UP AND CONTINUE TO *223*. OTHERWISE, GO TO *192*.

171 THIS DISTRICT IS CURRENTLY UNDER THE CONTROL OF THE SHADOW GUILD. IF ONE THE THIEVES HAS TAKEN REFUGE HERE, THE GUILD WOULD UNDOUBTEDLY KNOW. HOWEVER, YOU HAVE NOT YET MET THEIR LEADER, RUKMINI KALAM, AND YOU DOUBT THAT HE WOULD BE INCLINED TO HELP THE CITY'S AUTHORITIES. PROCEED WITH CAUTION.

172

THE THIEVES FINALLY LET YOU GO AND RECOMMEND YOU LEAVE THE AREA. IF NOT, THEY'LL HAVE LITTLE MERCY WHEN SHOWING YOU THE WAY...

GO TO *100* TO START HUNTING ONE OF YOUR OTHER TARGETS, IF THERE'S STILL TIME.

173

YOU'VE SEEN THIS SORT OF MAGICAL LANTERN BEFORE. IF YOU TEAR IT IN TWO IN AN ENCLOSED AREA, IT WILL EXTINGUISH ALL NEARBY ARTIFICIAL LIGHT. ADD THE *FOTO-FAJII* TO YOUR *INVENTORY*, THEN CLIMB THE BARRICADE TO CONTINUE TO *217*.

174

YOU LOSE *6 LIFE* POINTS *. DESPITE THE INTENSE PAIN, YOU MANAGE TO STAY ON YOUR FEET AND FLEE THE AREA. GO TO *217*.

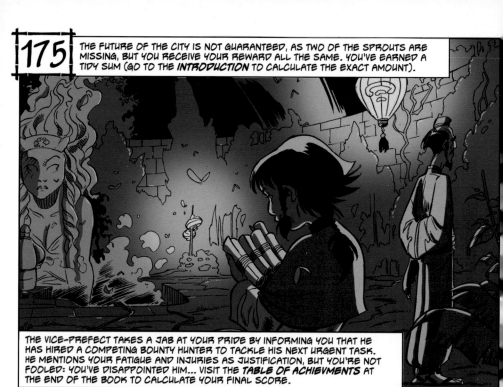

175 THE FUTURE OF THE CITY IS NOT GUARANTEED, AS TWO OF THE SPROUTS ARE MISSING, BUT YOU RECEIVE YOUR REWARD ALL THE SAME. YOU'VE EARNED A TIDY SUM (GO TO THE *INTRODUCTION* TO CALCULATE THE EXACT AMOUNT).

THE VICE-PREFECT TAKES A JAB AT YOUR PRIDE BY INFORMING YOU THAT HE HAS HIRED A COMPETING BOUNTY HUNTER TO TACKLE HIS NEXT URGENT TASK. HE MENTIONS YOUR FATIGUE AND INJURIES AS JUSTIFICATION, BUT YOU'RE NOT FOOLED: YOU'VE DISAPPOINTED HIM... VISIT THE *TABLE OF ACHIEVMENTS* AT THE END OF THE BOOK TO CALCULATE YOUR FINAL SCORE.

176 YOU ARRIVE AT THE SHADOW GUILD'S DEN. YOU'LL NEED EVERY LAST OUNCE OF YOUR CHARISMA TO CONVINCE THESE UNDERLINGS TO LEAD YOU TO THEIR MASTER.

IS RUKMINI THERE? WE HAVE SOMETHING THAT MIGHT INTEREST HER...

IF YOU HAVE A *GOLDEN BROOCH*, GO TO 227.
IF NOT, GO TO 202.

YOUR TROUBLES WITH THE SHADOW GUILD ARE OVER! YOU CAN HEAD TO ANOTHER DISTRICT AT *100* IF THERE'S STILL TIME, OR SET YOUR SIGHTS ON THE REVENANT AT *232*.

MMM... AND WHAT'S IN IT FOR ME?

GO TO *215* TO SAY: "I WILL REPORT YOUR ACTIVE CONTRIBUTION TO THE VICE-PREFECT."

OR GO TO *197* TO RESPOND WITH: "THE FATE OF THE WHOLE CITY IS AT STAKE."

THANK YOU! A THOUSAND THANK YOUS! I AM YOUR SERV--

IT'S FINE. *STOP.*

YOU KNOW, FOR AE--

BE QUIET BEFORE I CHANGE MY MIND!

CURSE THE DAY I MET YOU!

YOU HEAD BACK TO THE HEART OF THE CITY AT *100*.

180

THE ACRID ODOR OF SALTPETER AND SULFUR ASSAULTS YOUR NOSTRILS.

IT'S CLEAR NOW, THE ROOM YOU'VE MANAGED TO INFILTRATE IS YOUR FORMER LOVER'S HIDEOUT. THERE HE IS, SNORING AWAY. BEFORE PROCEEDING, DECIDE WHICH WEAPON YOU PLAN TO USE...

181

REMOVE THE *BLACK LOTUS* FROM YOUR *INVENTORY*. YOU CAN ATTACK THE ONI FROM THE SIDE AT *206* OR STAB IT IN THE LEG AT *230*.

182

223

190

183

TOK

TAK,,,

CRRRRR,,,

YES!! THE BARS SINK BACK INTO THE GROUND JUST AS THE PYROMANIAC WALKS INTO THE ROOM. FACE HIM AT *218*.

184

TOK TOK

NO ONE RESPONDS. YOU CAN PICK THE LOCK AT *213* IF YOU HAVE THE **BURGLARY** SPECIALTY. YOU COULD ALSO CLIMB UP TO THE WINDOW AT *231* OR GIVE UP ON SEEING GOZAN-BO AND GO TO *220*.

185 YOU SEE HIM, BUT HE DOESN'T SEE YOU. THE ADVANTAGE IS YOURS. YOU CAN LEAVE QUIETLY THROUGH THE OTHER DOOR AT *232* OR ATTACK THE JAILER AT *209*.

186

THAT SETTLES THAT. TAKE HIM CAPTIVE AT *222*.

187

188 LIAR! WE KNOW YOUR PAST WITH HIM! YOU CLEARLY HAVE AN ULTERIOR MOTIVE HERE.

A KNOCK ON THE HEAD COSTS YOU *1 LIFE POINT* ✻ AND YOU FIND YOURSELF AT *214*.

189

HEY! WHERE ARE YOU GOING?

OVER HERE, BOYS! INTRUDER!!

OH NO!

YOU PUT UP A FIGHT, BUT A KNOCK ON THE HEAD COSTS YOU *3 LIFE* POINTS ✳ AND YOU END UP AT *214*.

190

223

182

170

191

DON'T YOU WORRY, HE KNOWS ME.

CONVINCED OF YOUR GOOD STANDING WITH THE SHADOW GUILD, HE SHOWS YOU A SECRET PASSAGE THAT LEADS TO THEIR DEN, NEAR THE EAST GATE. YOU MAKE YOUR WAY THERE IMMEDIATELY AND FIND YOURSELF AT *176*.

192
IF YOU WERE HOPING TO FIND MEMBERS OF THE SHADOW GUILD, YOU CERTAINLY HAVE. THEY HELP YOU CLIMB OUT, BUT A CLUB TO THE HEAD COSTS YOU *1 LIFE* POINT *.
YOU REGAIN CONSCIOUSNESS AT *214*.

193
YOU DIDN'T HAVE TO WAIT LONG FOR YOUR SLEEPING DRUG TO TAKE EFFECT. REMOVE THE *FEMME FATALE* FROM YOUR *INVENTORY* AND OPEN THE DECORATED DOOR AT *180*.

194

I SHOULD HAVE KNOWN THAT THEY WOULD CALL ON YOU!

WHAT WILL YOU DO WITH ME?

I KNOW YOU. IF I LET YOU LIVE, YOU AREN'T GOING TO GIVE UP.

HE TEASES YOU FOR A LONG WHILE, BUT YOU TAKE IT IN STRIDE. IF HE'S STILL THE MAN YOU KNOW, HE'S FAR FROM BEING INFALLIBLE...

GO TO *216* TO RESPOND WITH: "I WOULD HAVE PREFERRED YOU WEREN'T INVOLVED IN THIS."

OR BEG IN *167* WITH: "I WOULD BE MOST GRATEFUL. MORE THAN YOU KNOW..."

THE OLD MAN BARELY WOKE BEFORE YOU JUMPED ON HIM. PUSHING AWAY THE FAINTEST REMORSE, YOU ADD THE *GOLDEN BROOCH* TO YOUR *INVENTORY* AND START CLIMBING THE STAIRS TO *176*.

SHE'S GIVING US THE RUNAROUND. PUT HER IN THE FRIDGE, RUKMINI!

A KNOCK ON THE HEAD COSTS YOU *1 LIFE POINT* ✳ AND YOU FIND YOURSELF AT *214*.

198

OOH! FEMME FATALE!

IF YOU STEAL THE VIAL, ADD THE *FEMME FATALE* TO YOUR *INVENTORY* AND DISAPPEAR BACK INTO THE STREET AT *187*. IF YOU REFRAIN FROM DOING SO, INTERROGATE SOMEONE AT *233*.

199

YOU'VE MANAGED TO GET LOST IN THIS MAZE OF SMELLY ALLEYWAYS, BUT YOU FINALLY SEE A LANDMARK. A BUILDING IN THE DISTANCE LOOKS FAMILIAR...

200

HOW MANY SPROUTS HAVE YOU RECOVERED?
NONE: GO TO *125*.
TWO: GO TO *150*.
FOUR: GO TO *175*.
ALL: GO TO *225*.

201

IF YOU ENJOY MAKING CRAFTS, THIS MIGHT BE OF SOME USE TO YOU. REGARDLESS, YOU DECIDE TO ADD THE *ANIMAL GLUE* TO YOUR *INVENTORY* BEFORE RETURNING TO *182*.

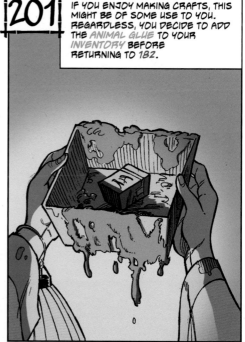

202

THE PYRO, EH? AND WHO HIRED YOU TO FIND HIM?

GO *178* TO RESPOND WITH "THE VICE-PREFECT. THE PYRO WENT A LITTLE TOO FAR THIS TIME..."

OR GO TO *188* TO SAY: "NO ONE. HE JUST HAS AN OLD DEBT TO HONOR."

203

THE EFFECT ONLY LASTS A FEW MOMENTS. YOU RUSH TOWARDS YOUR TARGET AND TAKE HIM WHILE HE IS REELING FROM THE SURPRISE. REMOVE THE *FOTO-FAJII* FROM YOUR *INVENTORY* AND GO TO *222*.

SCRTCH!

204

AFTER WANDERING A SHORT WHILE, YOU OBTAIN AN AUDIENCE WITH THE LEADER OF THE DERELICTS...

I WOULD LOVE TO HELP YOU, LITTLE ONE. WITH GREAT PLEASURE, EVEN! BUT THE GUILD MUST KEEP ITS SECRETS...

...ALTHOUGH YOU TAKE CARE NOT TO MENTION YOUR MISSION.

GO TO *191* IF YOU HAVE THE *STAR FISH*. IF NOT, GO TO *219*.

205 IF YOU HAVE ANY LEFT, YOU CAN ADD A DOSE OF *FEMME FATALE* TO THE BARREL AT *193*. YOU ARE FREE, OF COURSE, TO RETURN TO *232* OR CREEP STEALTHILY OVER TO THE OTHER DOOR....

206

YOU LOSE *4 LIFE* POINTS, BUT MANAGE TO PREVAIL VICTORIOUS. YOU DODGE THE REST OF HIS ATTACKS AND TEAR THE MONSTROUS BRIGAND APART AT *173*...

207 UNFORTUNATELY, THE PYROMANIAC SUDDENLY AWAKENS JUST AS YOU REACH THE DOORWAY INTO HIS ROOM. GO TO *218*.

MY SPIES CONFIRMED THAT A MINISTER OF SATTURU ORDERED THE THEFT OF NÜWA'S TEARS. IT WAS HIM THAT YOU SAW FLEEING MUBAN...

BUT MORE IMPORTANTLY, THE LEADER OF THE ARTISANS' GUILD IS WORKING FOR THE ENEMY, TOO! WHAT'S MORE IS THAT SHE LEFT THE CITY VIA THE NORTH GATE ONLY AN HOUR AGO, HIDDEN IN A PALANQUIN, ESCORTED BY 4 CAVALRYMEN. SUCH A FELON WILL SURELY LOOK FOR REFUGE IN SATTARU...

SINCE I HAVE NO PHYSICAL PROOF, I CAN'T VERY WELL SEND ANY LAW ENFORCEMENT AFTER THEM.

THE MOUNT WITH WHICH WE ARE ENTRUSTING YOU SHOULD ALLOW YOU TO CATCH UP TO THE CONVOY WITHOUT DIFFICULTY.

YOU MUST THEREFORE PURSUE HER IMMEDIATELY. KILL HER MEN, BUT RETURN HER TO THE CITY, ALIVE.

ADD ANOTHER *HEALTH POTION* TO YOUR *INVENTORY* (THIS ONE ONLY HAS A SINGLE DOSE), AND MAKE YOUR WAY TO *91*.

A KNEE TO YOUR STOMACH COSTS YOU *1 LIFE* POINT, BUT YOU MANAGE TO GET THE UPPER HAND.

THE PYROMANIAC! WHERE IS HE?

THERE, IN THERE--

232

YOU KNOCK HIM OUT, JUST IN CASE. HE HAD IT COMING TO HIM, AFTER ALL...

??

AN *ONI!*

RRRR...

ONLY A DOSE OF *BLACK LOTUS*, IF YOU HAVE ANY LEFT, WOULD GIVE YOU A CHANCE AT DEFEATING HIM. IF YOU CAN - AND WISH TO - USE THE POISON, GO TO *181*. OTHERWISE, GO TO *174* TO CLIMB THE BARRICADE.

211

THERE IS NOTHING TO HOLD ONTO BUT BROKEN GLASS. THE FALL BACK DOWN IS BRUTAL. RETURN TO *184*, WITH *5 LIFE* POINTS FEWER.

212

HE'S NOT LIKELY TO WAKE FOR THE NEXT FEW HOURS. GO TO *176* TO MAKE YOUR WAY UP THE STAIRS.

213

CLOSE THE DOOR, LITTLE MISS NOSY!

YOUR DIPLOMACY, PAIRED WITH HIS UNBRIDLED HATRED FOR THE PYROMANIAC, QUICKLY PUTS YOU IN THE RACKETEER'S GOOD GRACES...

WHICH IS WHY HE ENDS UP TELLING YOU WHERE YOU CAN FIND A SECRET PASSAGE TO THE SHADOW GUILD'S DEN, NEAR THE EASTERN GATE. YOU HEAD TO *176* WITHOUT FURTHER DELAY.

I STILL SEEM TO HAVE ALL OF MY THINGS, SO THEY CLEARLY AREN'T PLANNING TO LET ME ROT IN HERE THAT LONG.

KRRR

THE ONLY WAY OUT IS A LOCKED DOOR WHOSE HINGES APPEAR TO HAVE BEEN WEAKENED FROM YEARS OF HUMIDITY. GO TO *185* IF YOU HAVE THE **BURGLARY** SPECIALTY. IF NOT, YOU CAN KNOCK DOWN THE DOOR AT *226* OR WAIT A BIT AT *172*.

HMM... ACTUALLY, WE WOULD DO WELL TO IMPROVE THAT RELATIONSHIP.

NIXA! LEAD HER TO THE PYROMANIAC.

YOUR PREY HAS WITHDRAWN INTO A HOUSE ADJOINING THE GUILD'S DEN, BY PERMISSION OF RUKMINI. YOU MAKE YOUR WAY THERE AT *180*.

216

I HAVEN'T FORGOTTEN YOU EITHER. I'LL LET YOU OUT OF HERE AS LONG AS YOU PROMISE NOT TO ATTACK ME.

OF COURSE.

AE-CHA, ON THE OTHER HAND...

CLAC

CRRRR

YOU LOOK AT HIM ONE LAST TIME BEFORE HEADING BACK TO THE HEART OF THE CITY AT *100*. YOU COULD CHOOSE TO BETRAY YOUR WORD, AND ATTACK HIM AT *229*, OR USE THE *FOTO-FAJII* AT *203*, IF YOU HAVE ONE.

217

YOU CROSS PATHS WITH JALKO, AN OLD FRIEND WHO LIVES IN THE LOWER DISTRICT. HE SAW THE PYROMANIAC LAST NIGHT, BUT DOESN'T KNOW WHERE HE'S STAYING. HOWEVER, JALKO DOES GIVE YOU THREE DIFFERENT IDEAS OF HOW TO GET IN TOUCH WITH THE SHADOW GUILD.

YOU CAN VISIT GOZAN-BO, A RACKETEER CURRENTLY AT ODDS WITH THE SHADOW GUILD AT *184*; YOU CAN SPEAK WITH THE DERELICTS ASSOCIATED WITH RUKMINI KALAM AT *204*; OR YOU COULD TAKE A JOURNEY THROUGH THE SEWERS CONTROLLED BY THE GUILD AT *195*.

YOU!?

GO TO *229* IF YOU HAVE YOUR HANDS ON YOUR BUTTERFLY KNIVES, OR TO *186* IF YOU'VE CHOSEN THE MANRIKI. YOU CAN USE A *FOTO-FAJII* AT *203*, IF YOU HAVE ONE.

BAH! AFTER ALL, IT DOESN'T CHANGE ANYTHING! GO UNDERGROUND AND LOOK FOR A PORTCULLIS IN THE MAIN SEWER.

YOU'LL FIND AN ENTRANCE TO THE GUILD'S DEN ON THE OTHER SIDE.

AFTER A BRIEF THANK YOU, YOU LEAVE TO MAKE YOUR WAY TO *195*.

YOU CAN RETURN TO THE HEART OF THE LOWER DISTRICT TO SPEAK WITH THE DERELICTS WHO WORK FOR THE GUILD AT *204* OR LOOK FOR AN ENTRANCE THROUGH THE SEWERS AT *195*.

221 AN OPIUM FACTORY! OPIUM IS NOW ILLEGAL, AND FOR GOOD REASON, BUT THIS SORT OF THING EITHER DISAPPEARS TO THE LOWER DISTRICTS OR STARTS THERE IN THE FIRST PLACE.

222

WHERE ARE THEY? GIVE THEM TO ME OR *DIE!*

YOU HAVE WHAT YOU NEED, DARLING. PLEASE, LET ME GO! IF YOU DON'T, I'LL LOSE MY HEAD... OR A HAND, BEST CASE SCENARIO.

HEY! CAREFUL WITH THAT! IN THE LITTLE BAG, JUST UNDER MY SHIRT.

YOU CAN DELIVER HIM TO THE GUARD BEFORE RETURNING TO THE TEMPLE AT *100*, OR GRACIOUSLY FORGET ABOUT THE 1000 COINS REWARD YOU WOULD RECEIVE BY GOING TO *179*.

IN EITHER CASE, ADD THE *TWO SPROUTS* TO YOUR *INVENTORY*.

223

IF YOU HAVE THE *DISGUISE* SPECIALTY, YOU CAN MAKE USE OF IT AT *169*. IF YOU WOULD PREFER TO ENSURE THE GUARD'S SILENCE, YOU CAN GO TO *196*. OR YOU CAN TRY TO WALK BY WITHOUT HIM NOTICING AT *130*.

224

IMPOSSIBLE! AND NOW HE'S WAKING UP...

GO TO *183* IF YOU HAVE THE *WEAPON THROWING* SPECIALTY. IF NOT, GO TO *194*.

225 AS PROMISED, HERE IS YOUR PAYMENT. YET THERE'S MORE WHERE THIS CAME FROM... I HAVE A NEW MISSION, WELL SUITED TO YOUR ABILITIES, TO BE COMPLETED THIS VERY EVENING. IF YOU ACCEPT, YOUR PAYMENT WILL BE IN THE FORM OF A *JANJHAR* FORGED BY THE HIGH ENCHANTER, IN PERSON NO LESS. I MUST KNOW YOUR ANSWER THIS INSTANT, HOWEVER.

WE ARE SAVED!

A JANJHAR! AN ENCHANTED BRACELET OF GENUINE POWER -- WOULD IT BE THAT HARD? GO TO *208* IF YOU ACCEPT. IF NOT, HEAD TO BED AND ENJOY A WELL DESERVED REST, DREAMING OF YOUR NEWFOUND WEALTH (RETURN TO THE *INTRODUCTION* TO CALCULATE EXACTLY HOW MUCH WEALTH THAT IS).

226

9!!

THE DOOR COLLAPSES ON THE FIRST PUSH!

YOU LOSE *4 LIFE* POINTS *, BUT MANAGE TO HOLD YOUR OWN WELL ENOUGH TO CONTINUE THE FIGHT AT *209*.

OLD CURLY IS **DEAD!** THERE'S BLOOD EVERYWHERE!

LIES WON'T SAVE YOU NOW. YOU WILL KNOW MANY CRUEL PUNISHMENTS AT THE HANDS OF THESE VENGEFUL THIEVES BEFORE THEY FINALLY DECIDE TO LET YOU DIE.

HÉ!!

TCHAK

YOU LOSE **7 LIFE** POINTS #. FORTUNATELY, THERE'S A BAR TO BLOCK THE DOOR FROM THE OTHER SIDE, GIVING YOU SOME BREATHING ROOM TO SEARCH FOR THE PYROMANIAC AT **180**.

229

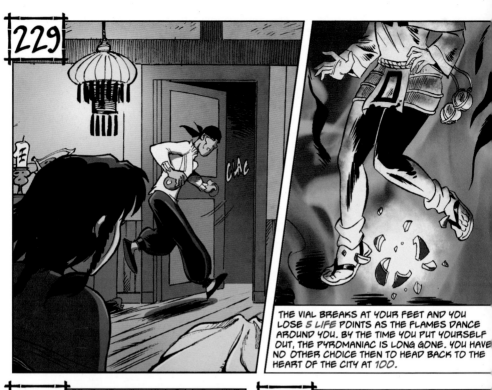

THE VIAL BREAKS AT YOUR FEET AND YOU LOSE *5 LIFE* POINTS AS THE FLAMES DANCE AROUND YOU. BY THE TIME YOU PUT YOURSELF OUT, THE PYROMANIAC IS LONG GONE. YOU HAVE NO OTHER CHOICE THEN TO HEAD BACK TO THE HEART OF THE CITY AT *100*.

230

NICELY DONE! YOU EVADE THE LAST OF THE WRETCHED BEAST'S WEAKENING ATTACKS BEFORE HE BLEEDS OUT AT *173*.

231

THIS COMPLICATES THINGS SOMEWHAT...

232

THE ELEPHANT CONTAINS *ROCK SALT*, A SUBSTANCE OF CONTROVERSIAL VIRTUE. YOU MAY ADD IT TO YOUR *INVENTORY* IF YOU LIKE.

233

YOU LEARN NOTHING OF THE THREE WHO DESECRATED THE TEMPLE, AND AS SOON AS YOU BREATHE A WORD ABOUT THE SHADOW GUILD YOU ARE ASKED TO LEAVE. BEST DO AS YOU'RE TOLD AND HEAD TO *187*.

234

235

YOU CAN ATTEMPT TO LAND A BLOW WITH YOUR LEFT BLADE AT *53* OR SWEEP HIS LEGS TO MAKE HIM FALL AT *116*.

TABLE OF ACHIEVEMENTS

IF YOU SURVIVED THAT DAY (AND, PERHAPS, EVEN THAT NIGHT) NOW IS THE TIME TO TAKE STOCK OF YOUR ACTIONS. SCORE THE APPROPRIATE NUMBER OF POINTS FOR EACH OF THE FOLLOWING ACHIEVEMENTS YOU ACCOMPLISHED DURING YOUR JOURNEY. THEN, ADD THEM TOGETHER TO OBTAIN YOUR FINAL SCORE.

GIVE THE *ANIMAL GLUE* TO THE CARPENTER : **+1**

OFFER THE *LINGLING-O* TO THE YOUNG GUARD : **+2**

FIND THE *PARRYING NECKLACE* : **+2**

INVESTIGATE THE MILL : **+1**

USE THE *FUMIGANT* : **+2**

SPEAK TO LUCILLE : **+1**

PLAY A MELODY WITH THE *FLUTE* : **+1**

FIND THE *DEFENSIVE AMULET* : **+2**

SOLVE THE RIDDLE OF THE ELEMENTS : **+1**

BRING THE *GARUDA* TO LIFE: **+2**

SOLVE THE RIDDLE OF THE STARS : **+1**